This book is dedicated to . . .

My son Apollo whom I love so much! He constantly gives with his heart to everyone he meets and reminds us all of the "real magic in this world". Thank you for making your Mom and I so very proud.

And

My good friend Alicia Riley. A wonderful mother, friend and "Biggest Bunny Lover of All". Thanks for all your support over the years.

Special Thanks to . . .

Mrs. Linda Winders. A close family friend and wonderful teacher to so many. Thank you for all your help with my books. God bless.

THE GREAT FOCUS POCUS

Written & illustrated by

Sneaky Boy®

Let me tell you a tale
from a long time ago
of a magical friend.
His name you might know.

Oh, this bunny is rare
and not easy to find!
He's a magical friend
with a heart that is kind.

But where is he from?
A good question indeed.
He is from a black hat,
and comes out when in need.

But to understand more,
you must hear the story
of the great "Focus Pocus"
and all of his glory!

So our story begins, such a long time ago,
with a boy, and a dream, and a magical show.

The Great Cosmo Ted was in town for a day.
All the children came out for his show and to play.

But one curious boy
wanted much more than this.
To meet his great idol . . .
a big chance not to miss.

As the show finished up,
people started to leave.
He hid by the back door
with some tricks up his sleeve.

As Ted quickly walked out,
the boy jumped in his way
with a cape and a wand
in a suit that was grey.

"My name, sir, is Mickey,"
he said ever so loud.
"I'll show you some tricks,"
as he kneeled down and bowed.

"I will soon make this coin
come straight out of my ear."
Then he suddenly tried,
but yet nothing appeared.

The Great Cosmo Ted
kept on smiling away
as Mickey kept trying
to surprise him some way.

He next tried a card trick,
but it didn't work out.
Mickey started to feel
some great sadness and doubt.

For his last final trick
would his wand disappear?
But again nothing happened.
In his eye was a tear.

"I am so sorry, sir."
He then lowered his head.
"I thought I could do this,"
as his face turned so red.

And then the magician
kneeled down beside him,
with an arm around Mickey
he then said with a grin,

"I know how you feel, son.
I was once like you too,
but a friend helped me out.
Do you want to know who?"

"This teacher showed me how
to be best in the world.
He's furry and witty
with his hair slightly curled."

Cosmo suddenly then,
took his hat off his head.
Then put it on Mickey's
and he quietly said,

"This hat belongs to you.
It will help you along.
Inside is a friend.
And his magic is strong!"

"When at home later on,
and you're sure you're alone,
flip the hat upside down,
and your friend will be shown."

Mickey wanted to thank
the Great Cosmo Ted,
but before he could speak,
the magician then said,

"Now remember these words
for the hat and its holder.
You must pass it onward
when you get older."

With a massive loud bang,
Cosmo Ted disappeared.
Leaving not but a trace
when the smoke had all cleared.

With his hat on his head,
he ran home oh so quick.
He now wanted to see
his new friend and his tricks.

So when Mickey got home
all alone in his room,
he then took off his hat,
and then . . . BAM . . . and KA-BOOM!

And who should be sitting
with the hat in his hand?
A furry grey bunny
with a smile so grand!

"I'm the Great Focus Pocus,"
said the bunny so proud.
"I am here to teach magic!"
A promise he vowed.

"I will show you the tricks
from the pros of the past.
With my guidance and teaching,
you will learn them so fast."

"To do this, I wink
and then shake my left ear,
and inside of your head,
the trick will appear."

"See, my job is to pick
the next magical whiz,
the one who will rise
to the top of the biz."

But Mickey just stood,
feeling ever so down,
with his hands at his sides
and his face in a frown.

"Are you sure I'm the one?"
Micky asked him with wonder.
"'Cause my tricks never work,
and today was a blunder!"

But the bunny just smiled
and said something so wise,
advice so magical,
it brought hope to his eyes.

"Your magical craft
takes more work than you think.
No such trick could be learned
in a simple, quick wink."

"Your true magic comes from
a belief within you.
Just keep trying your best
to see all your dreams through."

"You must focus your mind.
Concentrate on your goals.
Keep your nerves very calm.
And your thoughts in control."

"You must work at your craft,
and perfect it you must!
God gives us all talents
with great wisdom and trust."

"See, my job is to guide,
to help show you the way,
but the hard work is yours
at the end of the day."

"If you work very hard
and give all that you've got,
all your dreams will come true.
Fail—you will not!"

And with all those wise words
Mickey vowed to succeed,
to work hard at his craft
and become great indeed.

Focus Pocus worked hard
to help show him the way.
They practiced so much—
almost three times a day!

They did trick after trick
and great spell after spell.
Mickey's magic improved.
He was doing so well!

Then the days turned to months,
and the months turned to years.
And as Mickey worked hard,
his mind started to clear.

Then one wet rainy day,
his grey friend disappeared.
Mickey found a small note.
In his eye was a tear.

"Dearest Mickey," it read,
"It is time—I must go.
My work here is all done.
Let's get on with the show."

"The world is now set
for your talent and art.
Remember what I taught.
Perform always with heart."

"You are now the very best—
the very best that there is!
A true one of a kind!
A great magical whiz!"

"And if you should need me,
wink your eye, shake your ear.
The Great Focus Pocus
will then reappear.

Mickey now was aware
of what he had to do—
to work hard at his trade,
and see his dreams through.

Then he chose a new name,
a fine name all would know—
"The Mystical Mickey
and his Magical Show."

His new show became famous—
the most famous of all.
All the children came out,
both the big and the small.

But as years moved on by,
and young Mickey got older,
he could never forget
of the hat and its holder.

What he promised to do.
Who he promised to find—
a magician like him
with a heart that is kind.

So by chance, late one night, as his show winded down,
stood a small pretty girl in a golden silk gown.

"My name is Patricia—I am gifted and great.
Will you see just one trick? I will not keep you late."

She then bowed and knelt down, with her cheeks all aglow,
"Let me show you one trick that I do in my show."

But before she could start,
Mickey stopped her and said,
"I have something for you.
It goes right on your head."

"This fine hat is now yours.
It will help you along.
Inside there is a friend,
and his magic is strong!"

And with these final words,
he passed on his great hat
with his magical friend
inside just like that!

And then into the night
he chose to depart
as the next magician
got ready to start.

So now at a show
when a bunny appears,
just watch for that wink
and that shaking left ear.

If you're lucky and calm
and are willing to wait,
you might see Focus Pocus,
the mystic and great!

About the Author

Sean Vincent (Sneaky Boy) was born in Ottawa, Ontario, Canada, but grew up in Pickering just outside of Toronto. He attended George Brown College where he studied Graphic Design. Over the next 25 years, he continued to work in the Graphics Industry, specializing mostly in consumer packaging and branding.

Always an avid reader and sketcher with a limitless imagination, it was a dream of his to produce children's books that would be not only easy, entertaining and enjoyable to read, but that would also communicate a moral and simple message.

He works as a Creative Director for a display company in the Greater Toronto Area, but aspires to produce more children's books in his spare time. He is the happy father of four children and now resides in Richmond Hill, Ontario.

Please  Visit us

www.sneakyboybooks.com